I'm Emma. I'm 9 years old. I like to sing and read. I'm a vegetarian and I like to try new foods.

This is my brother, Joe. He's 7. He likes almost every sport. He likes to read comics and he loves to draw.

This is our family travel journal. I keep a journal for my grandma. She used to travel a lot because she was a reporter and she says that a trip is like a scavenger hunt. You look for new things and find out about them. Grandma took notes so she could tell stories to her friends. Now I'll be able to tell you my stories!

This time we came to China to visit some friends.

It's so interesting here!

the day we Arrived

We went exploring right after we checked into our hotel. We noticed right away that the streets were very busy and filled with people and cars, but also bicycles and bicycle rickshaws, which are like bicycle taxis!

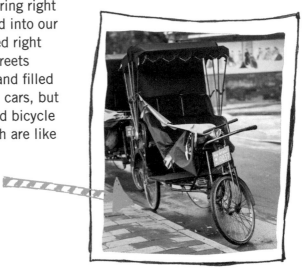

There were a lot of tiny shops with bright colors inside. I think red is the favorite color of China! There were red banners, red lanterns and red buildings. The desk clerk at the hotel told me that red is for good luck.

Cate's House

My friend, Cate, moved to China because her mom and dad got jobs here. We went to see them at their house today.

As we arrived, her neighbor came home from the market with a shopping bag. She was very friendly and stopped to say hello. She showed us the tea eggs she bought. They didn't look like any eggs I'd seen before! She explained that tea eggs are made by cracking the shells of hard-boiled eggs and soaking them in tea. After they were peeled, they reminded me of the quartz rocks we studied in third grade.

Cate's neighbor told us that 4 generations of their family live in one house! The woman who showed us the eggs is the grandma. Her mom, the great grandma, is almost 100 years old! After the neighbor left, Cate said that respecting and taking care of people older than you is very important in China. In fact, you should always say hello to the oldest person first when you are visiting someone. I usually say hello to the people my age first, so I'll try to remember while we're in China! When we went inside, I asked Cate who was older; her mom or her dad? I made sure to say hello to her older father first! So far, so good!

Cate's dad had brought home noodle soup for us from the market. There are lots of noodles here! While we ate, Cate's dad told us some more Chinese manners. He said you should pour someone else's tea before you pour some for yourself. If someone pours tea for you, you can tap two fingers on the table to say "thanks" (I guess that's if your mouth is full!). But the best one is that us kids can put the bowl right to our mouths and scoop the food in with our chopsticks. That was great news because I still can't pick up the food with chopsticks all the way from the table to my mouth!

fter lunch, we went to Cate's room to look at her stamp collection. She gave some to me, even though she only had a few. One has a serious looking man on it and both have some Chinese writing.

Here are the stamps Cate gave me!

Cate said that Chinese writing characters sometimes look like what they mean. I tried to guess what the writing meant. It's fun to try even if you don't know if you're right!

Cate showed me some.

The character for "mountain" looks like this:

The left side is traditional Chinese, and the right side is the modern way.

For the word "water" it looks like this:

水

For "sun" it looks like this:

日

found some flat blocks on Cate's desk and started to build a tower, but there weren't enough. But guess what? They weren't building blocks, but Tangrams, and they're for making pictures! With just those few shapes, we arranged them to look like a duck, a cat and a whale! We traced around the blocks so that I could have a set.

You can make a set too if you draw the shapes inside a square paper and cut them out.

See like this:

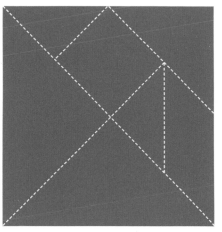

Then, rearrange them into the animals we made. You can find at least 100 shapes to make. It might be fun to see if you can invent a new shape, but it will be hard because people have been playing tangrams with these same 7 shapes for a very long time. The game was already very old when the first book about them was made in 1820!

the market

We visited Cate again today and we walked around town together. Since the market is close to their house, Cate's mom took us to see it. It has lots of little shops with everything you need.

The silk and embroidery shops had every color of the rainbow inside. The silk hung in rows from the ceiling to the floor. I just had to touch it. It was so soft and smooth. The shopkeeper gave me a piece of red silk ribbon to wear in my hair.

ear the door of an embroidery shop, Joe saw a picture of a cat that looked like our grandma's cat. When he went to look, it wasn't a photo or a painting, but embroidery. Someone had actually stitched the cat with thread! I could barely see the threads – they were so tiny! And guess what? When you looked on the back, there was embroidery of the back of the cat in just as much detail!

here are a lot of smaller stores here. Sometimes a store only sells one or two things. There was one store that only sold rice and soy sauce! The rice was in really big bags the size of my pillow at home. Rice is the most basic food here – maybe like bread or milk for us.

There were a lot of foods I'd never seen before. You should have seen the weird and wonderful fruits! A woman insisted that we try a longan. It was brown and bumpy like a tiny potato, and when she broke it open it was shiny and white. It smelled like a flower, but tasted like a grape. Longan means "dragon's eyes", and when it's peeled with the seed showing through the fruit, it really looks like an eyeball! Now when I eat them I'll be thinking about that, even though they're really sweet and delicious!

I saw a lot of long, skinny vegetables. There were long, skinny green beans (as long as my arm!), long, skinny eggplants, and a long, skinny, white radish. There was

something that looked like a giant cucumber – it was as big around as a watermelon. Even Cate's mom didn't know what it was!

I'm not used to seeing meat that still looks like the animal it came from, but here, the chicken still has the head and feet on and they sell every part of the pig (even the ears). I could hardly look at them, but Joe insisted on describing every detail out loud so that I had to plug my ears! There are also live fish, turtles, and frogs to take home to cook. I don't think my parents would even know what to do with a live fish if they took it home for dinner!

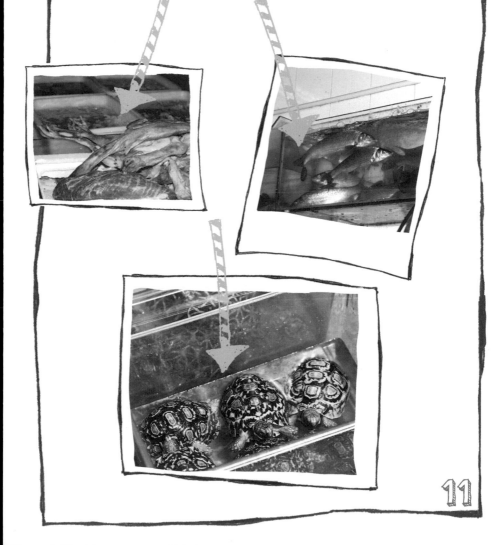

After looking at all that food, the smell of steamed dumplings from a nearby restaurant was irresistible. The cook served them from a giant, round, bamboo tray that rests on top of a pan of steaming water. The steam coming up through the tray keeps the dumplings soft and warm. We bought some and the cook handed them to us out the restaurant window. They were round, smooth and white, and when we ate them they were very soft, like a marshmallow, but the taste was like bread. Mine had shredded vegetables inside, and Joe's had pork. Cate's mom sat at a table to eat, but we went to sit under a weeping willow tree. The branches were so long they touched the ground like birthday streamers all around us.

While we were sitting there, two kids walked by with lollipops shaped like animals! We looked up the street and saw a man sitting at a table with a pot of hot syrup that he poured onto the cold marble table into whatever shape he wanted. I never saw that before.

As it started to get dark, I thought I saw birds flying over the canal, but Joe said "Those aren't birds. They're bats!" Before I could think about it, I put my hands over my head and ducked down. Cate laughed and said that even bats are good luck in China! Lucky bats? That's news to me!

Do you think bats are scary or cute?

The next day, walking along the canal, I saw something like the top of a giant gold scepter (you know, the stick a king holds) on top of a building. If they put gold on the roof, there must be more inside. I couldn't wait to go see.

The inside of the temple was so fancy, but not like a church at home. There were lots of gold statues inside. Back outside, there was a giant incense burner with incense sticks taller than I am! It smelled so strong I covered my face with my hand and went toward the street.

Lucky for me, just then a woman rode up on her bike which was carrying candied fruit on a stick and we bought some. The woman had wooden skewers of tiny apples soaked in sugar syrup and then covered with a shiny sugar glaze. The woman put the skewers into a tree-trunk shaped bamboo basket and they stuck out like the branches of a decorated Christmas tree. It was just like an old-fashioned ice cream truck! They were really beautiful and so sweet!

hile we were eating, we walked toward a statue of a warrior we saw near the temple. He looked scary to me because he was huge, had arching eyebrows like silkworms, and held a sword with a gigantic blade that made him look mean. He's a hero though, because he was really brave, he didn't brag, and he was loyal to his two best friends and helped them whenever he could. His name is Guan Gong.

I stayed behind to take a picture of myself looking fierce like Guan Gong, but Joe went to watch two kids flying kites. The kites looked like a fish and a dragonfly, and by the time I looked down to see the kids flying them, Joe had made friends and was holding one of the kites! They were cousins named Fai (the older boy) and Le (the younger girl). They said that it makes sense that kites have been in China for thousands of years because bamboo and silk both come from China and are both strong and lightweight. Good for flying!

school

Joe and I went to school with Cate today. She's really smart and adventurous so her parents let her go to the school close by their house even though she didn't speak Mandarin Chinese when she got here! She's learning Mandarin, but she said going to a school where she doesn't speak the language well is so hard, and she's really, really tired every day after school. But it should be worth it since Mandarin Chinese is spoken by many more people in the world than English!

Did you know that? I didn't.

The teacher let Cate translate into English for me even though we're not supposed to talk while the teacher is talking. The teacher said that in China, children learn to help the group before they help themselves. She told us a story about working together.

Once there was a kindly elephant looking for something to eat on a cloudy day. While looking for leaves and grass he saw a hummingbird, even smaller than usual, lying on her back with her feet in the air.

"What are you doing?" asked the elephant, thinking maybe the tiny bird had knocked its head and landed upside down.

"I've heard the sky will fall today, and I'm ready to hold it up", answered the hummingbird matter-of-factly.

The elephant looked up at the clouds, and although the elephant had lived a very long time, and had never heard that the sky could actually fall, he answered, "You are much too small to hold up the sky!"

"Well, you are right that I can't do it alone. But we should all do what we can, and this is what I can do." said the hummingbird hopefully.

And so, the elephant lay down by the hummingbird – the giant mammal and the tiny bird working together – waiting for someone else to come along.

It's kind of a silly story since the sky can't fall, but at least they wanted to help.

Cate's favorite part of the day is going outside for recess to play with her feather hacky sack. She showed us how to do it. You kick it up high with the side or top of your foot and try to keep it from hitting the ground. I've seen hacky sacks that are ball-shaped bean bags, but hers also has really bright feathers coming out the top. It looks a little like a dart stuck into a bean bag. Some people are really serious about it as a sport! There are rules and tournaments and everything!

Cate's friend, Qi goes everywhere with her feather hacky sack. She's even kicking while she's walking down the street.

During school, I saw Joe gazing outside at the soccer goal, so after school, he went right for the soccer game. He isn't shy. He was giving his teammates high fives within minutes of starting the game!

Cate says there are also outdoor ping pong tables. People love to play ping pong, but don't have space inside their houses for a table at home. So, they play outdoors at parks and restaurants.

gardens

In the evening, we went to see a fancy garden. This garden looked different than the ones I've been to. Instead of tons of plants with a few paths and a bird bath, there were just as many ponds, pavilions and rocks as there were plants. We read on the garden map that because the garden is small, every single thing was planned to make you feel peaceful.

The rocks looked like wet sand. If you squint your eyes when you look at them, they can look like animals. It's like looking at the clouds and seeing shapes. There was one rock that really looked like a lion! The rocks are from near here at Taihu Lake and they send the rocks to gardens all over the world! Can you believe a giant rock could be so special people would want to send it that far away to look nice in their garden?

The names of the garden buildings tell something about the place, like Listening to the Sound of Rain Pavilion, With Whom Shall I Sit Pavilion and Pavilion of Fighting Ducks. What a great idea to name your buildings! Joe thinks we should name our house, but House of Happy Craziness doesn't sound like a name that would lead to a peaceful life. There is a real Stay and Listen Pavilion, but I think it makes a good name for a school. Stay and Listen School.

The goldfish in the garden pond were mixtures of orange and gold. There were so many, that you couldn't see the water between them!

Goldfish are good luck.

Actually, a lot of things are good luck here and you see them everywhere once you know.

Bamboo is for living a long time.

Lotus is for purity. Lotus is the flower on a lily pad, and I think purity means being good all the time. Have you ever seen a tree in a pot? Here in China, they have teeny, tiny trees called Bonsai in pots. They would look great next to my dollhouse at home.

My grandma loves plants so I took lots of photos for her. There aren't too many flowers in the garden though since the rocks and buildings are more important. Grandma said that lots of flowers that we like to grow came from China first, like my mom's favorite flower, the peony.

The peaceful garden at night made me very sleepy.

I was happy to go to bed that night.

Did you ever hear about a big discovery that took a really long time and lots of hard work? Well, if you can believe it, I heard two stories about big Chinese discoveries that came from something falling out of a tree into someone's cup! That sounds easy.

Shen Nong was an emperor who knew about plants and science. Even 5,000 years ago, in the year 2737 BC he said everyone should boil water to make it safer. He was boiling water outside when a leaf fell into his water. He decided to taste the water. The leaf turned out to be a tea leaf and that was the first cup of brewed tea. No one is really sure if this is true because it was so long ago, but it sounds possible!

Do you ever drink tea? I like it with milk and sugar. Yum.

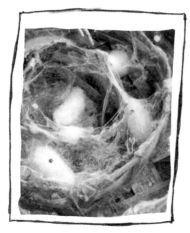

And since Shen Nong discovered tea, the empress Lei Zu could sit under a mulberry tree a hundred years later drinking her tea. A silkworm cocoon fell from the tree right into her tea. But, instead of throwing it away, she stopped to think about it and noticed the shiny thread unwinding in the hot liquid. She and her maid unwound the cocoon and then twisted several threads together and invented silk!

It's so strange that fabric that is shiny and smooth comes from bumpy gray silkworms! They eat only mulberry leaves for about a month. Then they spin their cocoon by making one long silk thread. The silk is really their dried spit, and that one thread can be half a mile long or more! After the Chinese figured out how to make silk, they kept it secret for thousands of years so they could be the only ones to make it. Can you imagine that something could stay secret for that long?

the Canals

Today was our day for a boat ride on the canals! The tour guide said that the canals are like roads! They were built so that things like rice and silk could go between towns by boat. They're so old that they were dug by people using shovels. That's hard to imagine because most of the canals are really deep and go for as far as I can see.

There are still some people who live on houseboats, but most of the boats are for people to take rides. The regular

houses are right next to the canal, just like if it was a street. There are stairs going down into the water and people use the water for washing clothes. I can't imagine seeing my neighbors at home washing their clothes in their front yard.

Everyone wants to be by the canal! Besides women doing chores, there are groups of men playing chess, fishing, or taking their pet bird or cricket for a walk.

Pet cricket? Yes!

They are green like peas and they eat tiny bits of fruits and vegetables. Their cages can be a plastic jar with holes for air, woven bamboo, or a hollow gourd. You buy them in a pet market in the spring and they only live for a few months. It would be sad to lose your pet after just a few months!

The pet birds are not usually the pretty ones, but the ones with a beautiful song, like the Mongolian lark. That lark doesn't have any fancy colors – only black, brown and white – but it sings a lot.

When we stopped to watch some ducks in the canal, we saw an old man painting a scene of the black and white houses. He laughed when we came too close to the ducks and scared them away. When he saw me looking at his painting, he took out a piece of paper and drew some ducks for me. He said ducks swimming in reeds symbolize good luck in school. Joe ripped out a page from our journal so he could give the man a drawing. But, Joe drew a picture of a duck superhero. The man smiled and put it next to his painting.

Here's what the Chinese artist drew.

Here's what Joe drew— SUPER DUCK!

My grandma told a lot of stories about the new foods she ate when she traveled. She told me she ate Roast Duck in the capital city of Beijing. (It came to the table roasted, but with the head still on, just like at the market!). The waiter cut the meat off and served it with green onion, sweet plum sauce and very thin pancakes. My grandma rolled everything up like a taco and said it was sweet and salty at the same time.

We went to a restaurant for a nice dinner on our last night in China. I looked at the menu and I was glad I didn't have to order!

What would you choose?

Now that we've been here a while, I've noticed something about the food. Most everything is cut into small pieces so you can pick up each piece with chopsticks. I don't need to cut my food at the table (I never like doing that at home). Have you ever tried chopsticks? It's hard! I saved a pair of kid's chopsticks so I can practice.

Luckily, some things you just eat with your hands, like crunchy fried spring rolls. Delicous.

My favorite soup here is Egg Drop Soup. The waitress told us that they make it by slowly pouring a string of mixed egg into broth. We got the recipe and you can try to make it!

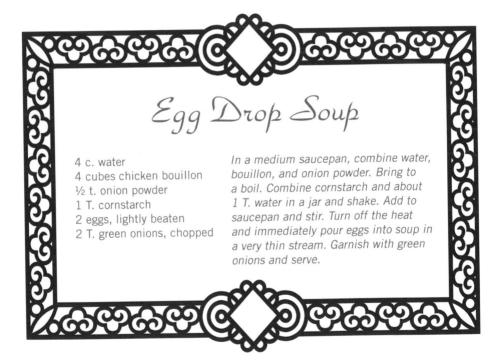

Egg Drop Soup

4 c. water
4 cubes chicken bouillon
½ t. onion powder
1 T. cornstarch
2 eggs, lightly beaten
2 T. green onions, chopped

In a medium saucepan, combine water, bouillon, and onion powder. Bring to a boil. Combine cornstarch and about 1 T. water in a jar and shake. Add to saucepan and stir. Turn off the heat and immediately pour eggs into soup in a very thin stream. Garnish with green onions and serve.

I'm not ready to go home yet, but school starts again soon. We only saw a tiny bit of China. It's about the same size as the US, but there are four times more people! I tried to imagine my town being four times more crowded, but I couldn't!

I gave Cate a picture I found at the market of two Chinese boys playing hacky sack, and Cate gave me a tiny book of postcards of China and some papercuts to do when I get home. A papercut is like a picture where you cut out the shape instead of drawing it.

You can make a copy of this Papercut and cut it out.

Leaving here is as hard as going to school knowing that I haven't finished a big project that's due. But, here's what Cate's mom told me the Chinese would say:

A journey of a thousand miles begins with a single step.

I guess that means I only have to take one step, and then another until we are on the airplane home. (And when I have a project due, just start and keep doing each part until I'm done, hopefully on time!) I can't wait to tell Grandma and my friends all the stories about our adventure.

THE END.

Written by Laura Barta

Copyright © 2011 Whole Wide World Toys, Inc.
Hershey PA 17033
www.wholewideworldtoys.com

ISBN-13:
978-1456380564

ISBN-10:
1456380567